This Little Tiger book
belongs to:

_____ _____

_____

_____

_____

For Freddy, my cheeky little penguin x
- G D

LITTLE TIGER PRESS LTD,
an imprint of the Little Tiger Group
1 Coda Studios, 189 Munster Road, London SW6 6AW
www.littletiger.co.uk

First published in Great Britain 2019
This edition published 2019

Text by Georgiana Deutsch
Text copyright © Little Tiger Press Ltd 2019
Illustrations copyright © Ekaterina Trukhan 2019
Ekaterina Trukhan has asserted her right to be identified as the illustrator
of this work under the Copyright, Designs and Patents Act, 1988

A CIP catalogue record for this book is available from the British Library

PERFECTLY POLITE PENGUINS

NOT!

Georgiana Deutsch • Ekaterina Trukhan

Little Tiger
LONDON

Penguins are ALWAYS perfectly polite.

Penguins always wait their turn.

They love sharing their toys.

And they NEVER forget to say please and thank you!

Oh, no. Someone's misbehaving again.

This is Polly.
Say hello, Polly!

Polly prefers NOT to be polite.
She says it's . . .

BORING!

Sometimes Polly interrupts.

Sometimes she forgets to think about how
the other penguins might feel.

And she really doesn't like picking up her toys!

All together we dance and sing.
It's time to tidy everything!

I LOVE
the tidy-up song!

NOT TIDYING
AGAIN?!

At dinnertime, Polly's manners go from bad to worse.
Especially when the penguins have . . .

. . . fishy snacks. Uh oh.

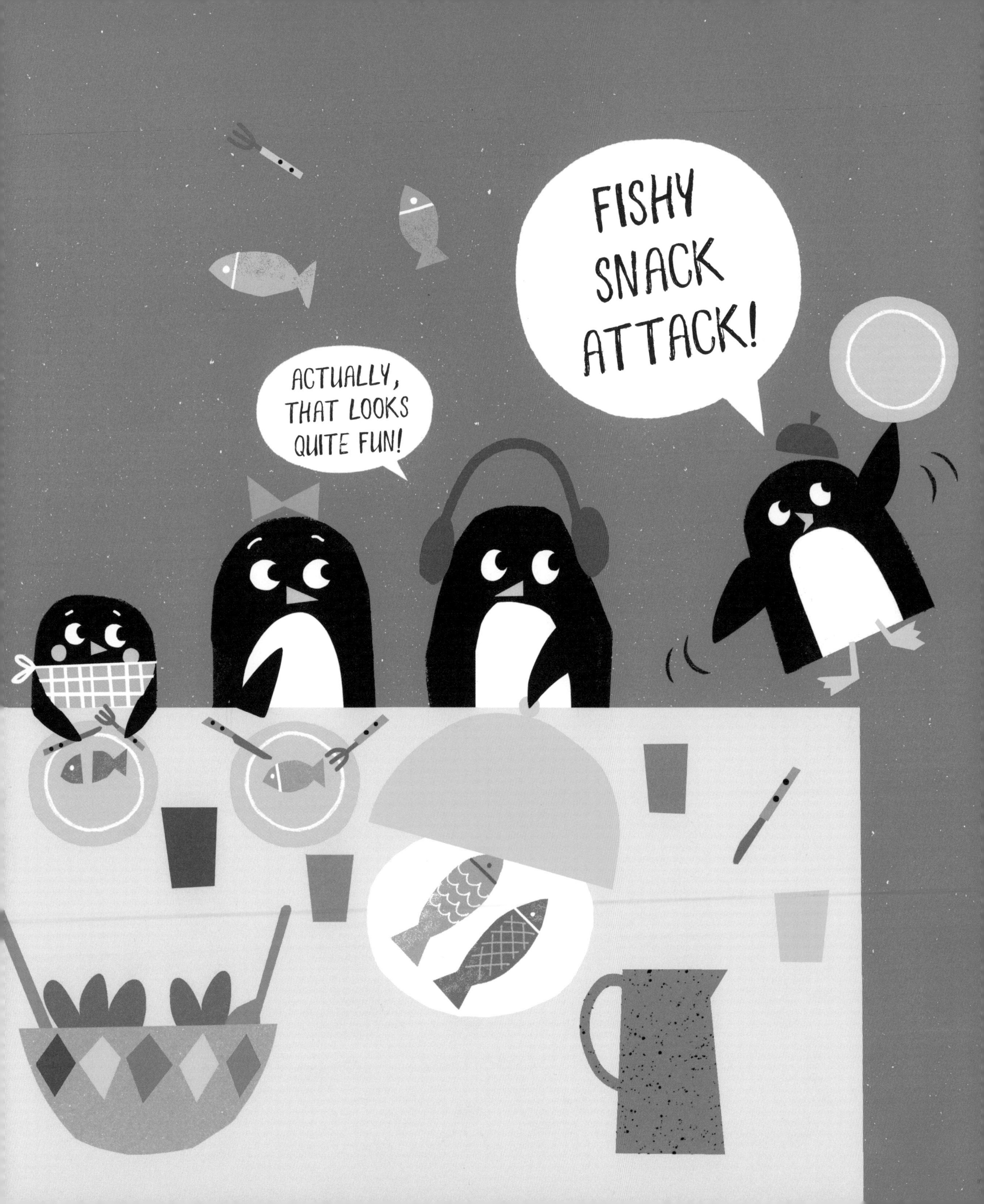
ACTUALLY, THAT LOOKS QUITE FUN!
FISHY SNACK ATTACK!

The perfectly polite penguins don't like it when Polly talks with her mouth full.

When she doesn't use her knife and fork.

And when she grabs the fishy snacks
without asking. Hang on a minute . . .

What's happened to all the perfectly polite penguins?

Oh. Where's Polly going?

Oh dear. Poor baby Peter
doesn't look very happy, does he?

Too noisy!

Luckily, Polly knows just how to make Peter feel better!

Don't worry, Peter. I've got an idea!

Well, that did the trick! Well done, Polly!

Perfectly polite penguins always clear up their toys together.

They always share nicely.

And they always think about how other penguins are feeling.

Even Polly the penguin is perfectly polite!

Well . . .

. . . most of the time!

FISHY SNACK ATTACK!

Where did that come from?

TEE HEE!

More perfectly FANTASTIC stories from Little Tiger Press!

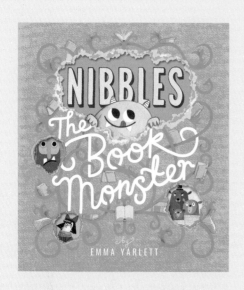

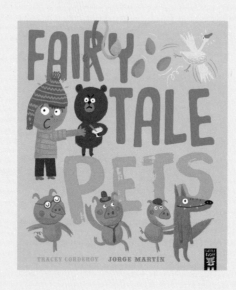

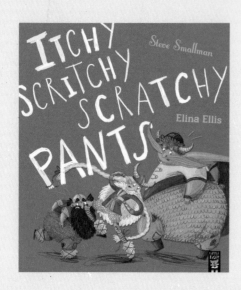

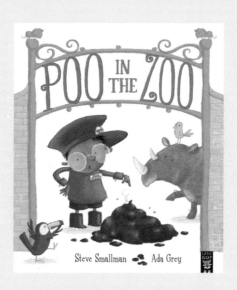

For information regarding any of the above titles or
for our catalogue, please contact us:
Little Tiger Press Ltd, 1 Coda Studios, 189 Munster Road, London SW6 6AW
Tel: 020 7385 6333 · E-mail: contact@littletiger.co.uk
www.littletiger.co.uk